For
Alexandra Rebecca
Diamond

Library of Congress Cataloging-in-Publication Data is available. Library of Congress Catalog Card Number 2009032485.
ISBN 978-0-7636-4878-7. Printed in Shenzhen, Guangdong, China. This book was typeset in ITC Esprit. The illustrations were done in acrylic.
Candlewick Press, 99 Dover Street, Somerville, Massachusetts 02144. Visit us at www.candlewick.com. 10 11 12 13 14 15 CCP 10 9 8 7 6 5 4 3 2 1

THE SHADOW

DONNA DIAMOND

CANDLEWICK PRESS